© Published by Peter Haddock Ltd., Bridlington, England. Printed in China.

The Little Angel
With Silver Hair

**Illustrated by Jenny Press, courtesy of
Simon Girling & Associates**

The Little Angel With Silver Hair

Once upon a time there was a little angel with beautiful, silver hair. She had been naughty and Saint Peter sent for her.

"Come here, naughty one," he said. "You do not seem to realise that everyone here in Heaven has work to do, especially at Christmas time. We all have to make someone on Earth happy."

She hung her head and Saint Peter frowned and said,

"But **you** have been lazy and can no longer stay with us. So, off you go - you must go down to Earth and make someone happy. Until you do, you will not be allowed back to Heaven!"

So the little angel found herself outside the gates of Heaven wondering what to do. Down to Earth she flew and found everything covered in a blanket of snow. She was very cold in her thin clothes.

"Good afternoon," called out a rabbit as it hopped by leaving deep pawprints.

Suddenly there was a sound of sleighbells and into view came Santa Claus.

"Hello, little angel, and what are you doing on Earth?"

She hung her head in shame and confessed she had been lazy and naughty in Heaven.

"Well, come and do some work for me," said Santa. "Hop on the sleigh and I'll tuck you in."

After a while Santa stopped the sleigh and chose some splendid, green Christmas trees. Then he emptied out of his sack tinsel, toys and Christmas decorations.

"Would you like to help me decorate these Christmas trees?" he said.

"Oh, yes please!" said the little angel with a big smile.

"Good," said Santa. "I'll do the tops and you can decorate lower down."

They set to work and soon all the tinsel and toys were used up. Santa went to get some bigger presents and promised to collect her on his return.

The little angel suddenly noticed that one little tree had no decorations. Whatever could she do?

Suddenly she had a good idea. There were shining, golden stars on her dress and she took them off and hung them on the branches. What else could she use? Oh yes! Strands of her beautiful hair. She draped these round the tree and it looked really lovely when she had finished. Even the deer came to admire it.

When Santa came back he said,

"That was a very loving thought," and patted her kindly on the head. "Now, we must take these trees to the nearest village and perhaps you can find someone to whom you can take your little tree."

So Santa and the little angel went on the sleigh across the snow until they saw the lights of the next village twinkling in the distance. They stopped in the centre and Santa delivered all his presents.

The little angel did all she could to help until at last the time came for her to deliver the Christmas tree decorated with her shining, golden stars and her silver hair.

She carried the tree to a house where three good children lived. They were helping their mother to wash up as the angel tip-toed into the house and left the lovely tree as well as some presents.

She peeped through the window as the children danced with delight when they saw the tree and presents.

"Isn't it lovely! Someone very kind has left all this for us."

The little angel smiled happily and ran to join Santa in the sleigh.

"Now where do you want me to take you?" Santa asked.

"Please, would you take me back to exactly where you found me and then I can fly straight back to Heaven?"

"Right," said Santa, setting off. "Thank you for all your help and I'll make sure Saint Peter hears about it."

"Thank you and goodbye," called the little angel as she flew off.

When the little angel arrived back at Heaven Saint Peter was waiting.

"**Now** what have you been doing?" he asked. "Just look at your hair and where are your golden stars?"

When the little angel told him what had happened to her hair and stars, however, Saint Peter was very pleased with her and said,

"Now you can come back into Heaven."

He was so pleased with the little angel that he gave her some more golden stars and the older angels stitched them on to her robe for her.

As for her lovely, silver hair . . . well, that will grow again!